Puffin Books
WORZEL'S BIRTHDAY

How many birthdays does a scarecrow have every year?
Worzel doesn't really know – but he's sure that his *Bestest*
Birthday is just about to happen. And when his
sweetheart, Aunt Sally, comes back to the village, it really
does seem that this will be his Bestest Birthday after all.

But, sadly, Aunt Sally doesn't feel the same for Worzel.
All that interests her is the wonderful cake which John
and Sue have bought for him as a special treat!

Worzel's Birthday, which ends happily when Worzel
gets both a cake *and* a dance with Aunt Sally, has been
specially written for younger admirers of the rascally
scarecrow, and is based on two episodes of the
phenomenally successful television series.

Also available in Puffin for readers of six to eight is
Worzel Gummidge at the Fair.

Worzel's Birthday

Keith Waterhouse and Willis Hall

Based on the characters created by Barbara
Euphan Todd

Illustrated by Andrew Skilleter

PUFFIN BOOKS

Puffin Books, Penguin Books Ltd, Harmondsworth,
Middlesex, England
Penguin Books, 625 Madison Avenue,
New York, New York 10022, U.S.A.
Penguin Books Australia Ltd, Ringwood,
Victoria, Australia
Penguin Books Canada Ltd, 2801 John Street,
Markham, Ontario, Canada L3R 1B4
Penguin Books (N.Z.) Ltd, 182–190 Wairau Road,
Auckland 10, New Zealand

First published 1981

Made and printed in Great Britain by
Richard Clay (The Chaucer Press) Ltd,
Bungay, Suffolk
Set in Monophoto Plantin

Chapter One

John and Sue were swinging on one of the gates that led into the yard of Scatterbrook Farm. It was a sunny morning but the children couldn't agree about how they were going to spend it.

'Well, I don't *want* to play in the barn,' Sue said, crossly. 'I'd rather go to Ten-acre Field. I want to see Worzel.'

John made a face. Ever since the Crowman had brought Worzel back from the fairground, leaving Worzel's beloved Aunt Sally behind, Worzel had been very miserable indeed and no fun to play with.

'I don't want to talk to a scruffy old scarecrow,' John said. 'I've built a swing in the barn. We can have some fun there.'

'We can have some fun with Worzel,' Sue insisted. 'I'm going to Ten-acre Field.' She jumped off the gate and headed across the farmyard to Ten-acre Field, where Worzel Gummidge was supposed to be on duty in all winds and weathers, scaring the crows away from Mr Braithwaite's best corn. The children knew very well that he often left his place but, luckily, Mr Braithwaite himself had yet to find out.

John hesitated. He really wanted to try out the swing he had built in the barn by hanging a piece of stout rope from the roof and tying an old tyre to it. But on the other hand, whatever he might say, there was always the chance of some excitement with Worzel, because you never knew what he'd get up to next.

He hesitated only for a moment. Then he gave in and followed Sue. The two of them were racing across the farmyard when a voice stopped them.

'Hey! You two scallywags – where do you think you're running off to?' It was Mr Braithwaite, the farmer, who had come out of the farmhouse with his wife.

'We're going to Ten-acre Field,' John replied. 'We're going to see Wor –'

Sue dug him in the ribs and he stopped himself just in time. It would never do for any of the adults – not Mr or Mrs Braithwaite, or John and Sue's father, Mr Peters – to find out the children talked to a scarecrow who came alive.

'We're going to see whether there are any blackberries,' Sue put in, to explain John's pause.

'At this time of year?' Mrs Braithwaite exclaimed. 'You'll be lucky!'

Mr Braithwaite looked disapproving. 'Before you go looking for anything,' he said, 'you can nip across to that barn and tidy it up a bit.' He pointed to the barn where John had built his swing. 'I don't know what you've been doing in there but it's a terrible mess. Looks as if a scarecrow's set up home in it.'

The children were disappointed, but they knew they'd have to do what Mr Braithwaite asked.

'And by the time you've finished tidying the barn,' Mrs Braithwaite added, in a kinder voice, 'it'll be

6

time for elevenses. Home-made scones and apple flan.'

The children cheered up immediately. 'Come on,' John said, and they scampered off towards the barn. They arrived breathless at the door.

'*You* win,' Sue said. 'I wanted to see Worzel, not play in the barn.'

John pushed open the barn door and glanced inside. He turned back to Sue with a grin on his face. 'You've won, Sue. Worzel's here.'

And sure enough, there in the middle of the barn, sitting on John's makeshift swing, was Worzel Gummidge. He was looking happier than he had looked for weeks and was clearly enjoying swinging backwards and forwards on the old tyre.

Worzel looked up as the two children entered. ''Ullo, you three,' he said. 'Where is it then?'

The children were puzzled. They had no idea what Worzel was talking about.

'Where's what, Worzel?' Sue asked.

'Me prezzie,' Worzel replied.

'But why should we bring you a present, Worzel?'

'Because it's his birthday, I suppose,' John put in. 'It's *always* his birthday.'

Worzel was indignant. 'No, it ain't then, Mister Clever-Clogs,' he said, giving himself another swing on the tyre. 'But it *will* be my birthday soon enough. So where's my prezzie?' He stopped swinging and stared at the children. ''Tis better to be safe than bumswizzled, as the saying sez. So 'and it over.'

John was not impressed. 'I told you it was always his birthday, Sue.'

'An' I told you it worn't,' Worzel snapped back. 'Anyways, us scarecrows does 'ave more birthdays than you yewmans does. That's 'cos bits of us get born at different times, that's why 'cos that is.'

Sue thought Worzel was likely to start sulking soon so she asked politely, 'How many birthdays do you have, Mr Gummidge?'

'Seven, Missy.'

Sue's jaw dropped. 'Seven! Golly!'

'Scarecrows 'as always 'ad seven birthdays,' Worzel continued, 'for as long as –' He thought for a moment. 'For as long as there's been scarecrows they's 'ad seven birthdays,' he decided. 'We 'as a birthday for each leg – one for each arm, one for the stummick an' another for our 'ead.'

'Go on.' John was counting the number of birthdays off on his fingers.

' 'Ow do you mean, "go on"?' Worzel asked. 'Ain't nothin' to go on with. I's finished.'

'But that's only six,' John said.

'No, it ain't,' Worzel answered, starting to look sulky.

'Yes, it is,' John replied, showing Worzel how he counted them off on his fingers. 'Two legs, two arms, one stomach and one head. That comes to six.'

'Are you sure about that?' Worzel asked suspiciously.

' 'Course I'm sure,' John answered. Arithmetic was one of his best subjects.

'He's right, Worzel,' Sue put in. 'It *is* six.'

'Oh.' Worzel was disappointed but soon cheered up again. 'Like I was sayin' – scarecrows 'ave always 'ad six birthdays. Long as ever there's bin scarecrows they's 'ad six birthdays. Six. No more, no less.' He stopped and looked doubtful. He turned to John hopefully. 'Is six more than seven?'

'Of course not,' John replied. 'It's less.'

Worzel looked disappointed again. 'Pity, that,' he muttered. But he wasn't going to be put off so easily. After all, the thought of his birthday had been cheering him up for losing Aunt Sally. 'But a scarecrow's Bestest Birthday,' he continued, 'is the one they 'as for their 'ead. 'Cos when their 'ead is made, that's when they gets life breathed into 'em by the Crowman. An' that's what it's called – the Bestest Birthday.' He paused. 'An' that's what my next birthday is – my 'ead's birthday. My bestest one.' He looked proudly across at the children to see if they were as impressed as he was.

'When is it, Worzel?' Sue asked.

'When's what?'

'Your best birthday? What *date* is it?'

Worzel's face was blank. 'Don't know nothin' about dates now, do I?'

'Couldn't you look on the calendar?' Sue suggested.

'Oh arr, I could do that all right,' Worzel agreed. 'But it wouldn't do no good, seein' as 'ow I can't read.'

'But I thought you had a reading head?' John

asked. Both the children knew that Worzel had a supply of different heads he could put on if he needed and John was sure he remembered hearing about a reading head one day.

' 'Course I 'as a reading 'ead,' Worzel replied. 'I wouldn't be without it. But 't'wouldn't be no good for me to put my reading 'ead on to look for when my Bestest Birthday is. 'Cos it's my Bestest Birthday for the 'ead I got on now we're talkin' about. My readin' 'ead would 'ave an altogether different day for its Bestest Birthday, wouldn't it now?'

Sue thought for a moment. 'But if all your heads have got birthdays, Worzel, you must have more than six.'

'Is that a fact?' Worzel stared.

Sue nodded firmly.

'More than seven as well?'

'Tons more than seven'

Worzel grinned with pleasure. But not wanting to push his luck too much, he repeated: 'My bestest birthday of them all, though, 'as to be for the 'ead you're talkin' to. An' that's the birthday as is coming up.'

'But you've just told us you don't know when that is,' John said.

'Maybe not,' Worzel replied. 'But I *will* know, won't I?' He looked at the children's puzzled faces. 'What do you take me for? Think I'm daft or something?'

'Aren't you going to tell us?' Sue asked.

'Couldn't tell you if I wanted to,' Worzel

answered. ' 'Cos it's a secret, isn't it? Even from me.'

'Suits us,' John put in, rather crossly. 'If we don't know when it is, we won't have to give you any presents, will we?'

Worzel nearly fell off the swing with disgust. 'That'd just serve you right, you titchy yewman,' he said, grandly. ' 'Cos if you ain't going to give me no prezzies, you ain't goin' to get to come to my birthday party, is you?'

Sue sighed. 'How *can* we come to your birthday party, Worzel, if you won't tell us when it is?'

'Not "won't", missy,' Worzel replied. ' "Can't". 'Cos even I don't know, do I? But I can *show* you, if you promise not to let it on to nobody else.'

The children gave each other a puzzled look. It all sounded very mysterious, but for once Worzel really did seem to be telling the truth.

'All right, Worzel,' John said. 'Show us.'

A few minutes later, they found themselves standing with Worzel in the middle of a small meadow. There was nothing to see except the green grass of the meadow all around them.

' 'Ere 'tis then,' Worzel announced, stretching out his straw arms to take in the whole meadow.

'I can't see anything,' John said in a puzzled voice.

'Me neither,' Sue added.

' 'Course you can't see nothin',' Worzel said indignantly. 'There ain't nothin' to see. That's 'ow I know it ain't my Bestest Birthday yet. But when it *is* my Bestest Birthday – my oh my! – then you'll see somethin' then.' His eyes filled with wonder. 'Then you'll see somethin' rare enough to make your stummick tickle.'

The children stared at each other. They stared at the empty meadow. They stared at Worzel. They began to wonder whether the loss of Aunt Sally had made Worzel lose what little brain he had. They couldn't understand how anyone's stomach could tickle at the sight of anything. Or how Worzel's Bestest Birthday would ever come about.

Chapter Two

Later that morning, when the children had tidied up the barn and filled themselves with Mrs Braithwaite's tasty scones, they decided to walk down to the railway station to see how their father was getting on. Mr Peters had taken a temporary job as a parcels clerk, while the man who normally worked there was away on holiday. It was only a small, quiet village railway station but Mr Peters found it harder work than he expected. He had to make sure all the parcels that came by train were safely stored away in his office and handed over in one piece to the village people who came to collect them. There were more problems in that than Mr Peters had bargained for.

The children found him mopping his brow and arguing with Mr Shepherd. At first the children only half listened to what the bad-tempered old man was saying. They just enjoyed watching him getting crosser and crosser while Mr Peters got more and more flustered. But they started to listen more closely when they realized Mr Shepherd was trying to describe a parcel he was expecting.

'She's – well – she's that high,' Mr Shepherd was saying, waving his arms about vaguely, 'and she's sort of that shaped and –' He gave up as he saw Mr Peters' blank face. 'She's an Aunt Sally, that's what she is. You've seen her in fêtes often enough. She got pinched and now she's being sent back.'

The children gasped. What would Worzel do when he knew Aunt Sally was coming back? Mr Peters had a more immediate worry. He had no idea what Mr Shepherd was talking about. And at that particular moment the only thing standing in the parcels area was a grandmother clock with a ticket label on it.

'I'm only temporary here,' he explained to Mr Shepherd, 'but I really can't see anything that fits your description. There's this grandmother clock of course. Is that any relation?'

The children giggled quietly but Mr Shepherd was not amused. 'I don't want no grandmother clock,' he replied. 'I wants my Aunt Sally!'

Mr Peters sighed. 'Are you *sure* you've got the right department, Mr Shepherd? This is parcels. If she's your Aunt Sally, won't she be travelling in a carriage like everybody else?'

Mr Shepherd got crosser. 'She's not my Aunt Sally!' he protested. 'At least, she *is* my Aunt Sally in that she *belongs* to me. But she's not my Aunt Sally so's I'm her nephew, if you follow me.'

'Not quite, Mr Shepherd.' Mr Peters had never been to a fairground and never thrown a wooden ball at an Aunt Sally there so he had no idea what Mr Shepherd was talking about.

'She's *an* Aunt Sally. She's a valuable antique.' Mr Shepherd saw he was getting nowhere. He gave a sigh. 'Never mind. I'll come back next week.'

He left the parcels office in a very bad mood.

'There's a train due in very shortly, Mr Shepherd, she might –' Mr Peters started to call after him but Mr Shepherd was already out of hearing. Mr Peters mopped his brow again and turned to face his children. John and Sue were excited by the thought of Aunt Sally's return and amused by the state their father had got himself into.

'What are you two stood there sniggering at?'

'Nothing, Dad,' the children replied.

'Well, don't hang around here under my feet then. I've enough on trying to learn the ropes. This is a parcels office, not a place for kids to play.'

'By Gad, you're right, sir.' The speaker was a large, fierce man with a big red face who had just entered. Although he was dressed in ordinary clothes, the children could see from his stiff and upright bearing that he must have served in the army at some time.

The man looked at the children in an unfriendly way. 'Ought to be in school, the pair of you,' he growled. 'What you both need is six of the best.' He turned to Mr Peters for approval. 'I should think their father has a lot to answer for, don't you?'

'That is our father,' John pointed out.

'Humph!' The man eyed Mr Peters from head to toe and clearly decided he didn't approve of him after all. Mr Peters smiled weakly and asked if he could help.

With much huffing and puffing, the fierce gentleman introduced himself. His name was Colonel Bloodstock. He had long ago retired from the army and now he'd bought the Hall from Mrs Bloomsbury-Barton, who'd decided to move on. The Colonel's wife was dead so he'd be living in the Hall alone but he didn't mind that. This was partly because he didn't like people anyway, but partly because he planned to spend his time hunting, fishing and shooting.

'Some of me personal possessions are coming by rail,' he told Mr Peters. 'Any sign of 'em? It's getting a bit urgent.'

Mr Peters looked at the parcels area, which still only had one object in it. 'There wouldn't be a grandmother clock, would there, Colonel, among your . . .'

But he didn't finish. 'Grand*mother* – clock!' the Colonel roared. 'Of course not! Do you think I'm a sissy?' And the Colonel went into a long angry speech about how good transport was when he was with the army in India and how long it took British Rail to move a few bits and pieces from his old home in Basingstoke.

'Three weeks I've waited,' he grumbled. 'So when my things do arrive, I want them up at the Hall immediately. Understand?'

'Yes sir!' Mr Peters had to stop himself from saluting like a soldier. He started to tell the Colonel that a train was due in shortly, but the Colonel had already stormed out of the office, waving the children aside in a cross and bossy way. John and Sue decided they didn't care for Colonel Bloodstock.

Almost as soon as the Colonel was gone, Mr Peters heard the sound of a train coming into the station.

He straightened his British Rail porter's cap in a self-important way. 'Skedaddle, you two,' he said to his children. 'I've got work to do.'

In fact, Mr Peters had more work to do than he expected. The goods van of the train was filled to bursting with things to be unloaded. The train moved out, leaving the sweating Mr Peters with a huge pile of objects all over the platform, waiting to be taken into the parcels office. It wasn't difficult to guess that nearly all of these things belonged to Colonel Bloodstock. There were native carved masks. There were tigerskin rugs. There were the heads of animals, shot by the Colonel, which had been stuffed and mounted on wood. There was even an elephant's foot, which had been made into an umbrella stand. Mr Peters could see at once that the Colonel had spent most of his time in the army in India and Africa.

John and Sue watched in secret from the far end of the platform as Mr Peters went off to collect a handcart on which to start loading the Colonel's possessions. The children had been told to keep out of the way so they couldn't really offer to help, but they were very curious to see what was on the train.

Mr Peters returned and started to load spears and shields and rugs on to his handcart. Sue and John gave a little gasp. One of the parcels was very different from all the others, which were neatly wrapped and labelled. This one was badly wrapped in brown paper and cardboard. At present it was stuck head down inside the elephant's foot umbrella stand. But the children had no difficulty in guessing what was inside. It was Aunt Sally. Aunt Sally stiff and wooden, with her legs in the air, but Aunt Sally nevertheless. The children held their breath, wondering what to do.

By the time Mr Peters had finished, the small parcels office was almost completely filled with Colonel Bloodstock's belongings. Mr Peters felt very satisfied with how neat everything was and glanced at his watch. It was later than he expected. 'Blimey!' he said. 'I'll miss my lunch if I don't hurry. The pub shuts in five minutes.'

After all his hard work Mr Peters needed a drink, so there was no time to lose. He came out of the parcels office into the station entrance, locking the door behind him to stop anyone getting in from the street while he was away.

The children, still hidden, watched him go. They knew they had to move quickly if they were to help Aunt Sally. Luckily, there was another door to the parcels office from the platform itself. That was never locked and the children were able to sneak into the office that way without the sleepy old ticket collector noticing anything.

When they entered, they could see no sign of Aunt Sally amidst the pile of other parcels. Then they heard a sniffling sound and after that, a small voice crying: 'Help me! Oh – *please* – help me!' The children knew at once that Aunt Sally was no longer wooden. She had become alive again and was somewhere in the office. Then Sue spotted the clumsily wrapped parcel, now lying on its side, but with the head still firmly stuck inside the elephant's foot umbrella stand. No wonder Aunt Sally's voice sounded faint.

John took a grip on the elephant's foot. 'You take hold of Aunt Sally's legs and pull,' he told Sue.

He held tight on the elephant's foot and Sue pulled hard and in the end they managed to get poor Aunt Sally's head out. They stood her upright and pulled back the wrapping paper to reveal Aunt Sally's face. She looked very sorry for herself. Tears streamed down her face.

'The shame of it,' she cried. 'I've never travelled in such an undignified manner in all my carved life.'

'Where have you been, Aunt Sally?' Sue asked. 'And aren't you glad to be back?'

'Glad to be back?' Aunt Sally replied sniffily. 'In this dump? After the elegant life I've been leading! Glad to be back? Huh! I should cocoa!' Even through her tears, Aunt Sally managed to look very displeased indeed at being back. 'As to where I have been,' she continued proudly, 'I could tell you stories that would set your hair on end. The adventures! The excitement! The romance!' Aunt Sally gave a big dreamy sigh. 'I have been wooed by a circus strong man with shiny black hair and a black moustache.'

'Does Worzel know?' John asked. Worzel had told the children nothing about his adventures at the fair. All they knew was how much he had been missing Aunt Sally.

'*Worzel?*' exclaimed Aunt Sally, making a face.

20

'What could an iggerant scarecrow know about *my* innermost feelings? Why, I could write a book about it. Leastways,' she added, 'I could if I wasn't tied up like a flippin' 'at-stand. *Me* in a guard's van! An Aunt Sally what is used to travelling first class with dukes and duchesses being carried as baggage with my 'ead stuck in a smelly old elephant's foot.'

She would have gone on longer about her terrible journey if she hadn't seen all the other parcels. 'Where's all this lot going anyway?' she asked.

'To the Hall,' Sue replied. 'Mrs Bloomsbury-Barton's left and it's been bought by a Colonel.'

'A Colonel!' Aunt Sally's eyes lit up at once. 'A person of breeding in the village at last! Why, a colonel's almost as grand as a prince of the royal blood or . . . or . . .' A thought suddenly crossed Aunt Sally's mind. 'Where am *I* being sent?' She squinted down at the luggage label on her parcel but was unable to read what was there.

'Well?' She looked questioningly at the children.

'Back to Mr Shepherd's,' Sue said quietly.

'Oh no!' All Aunt Sally's grandness disappeared in a moment and tears came back into her eyes. 'Not back to that awful trunk? Not that 'orrible attic? Help me – *please*.'

'But Mr Shepherd's expecting you,' John said. He knew how badly Aunt Sally had treated Worzel and wondered whether the best thing might not be for her to go back to the trunk in Mr Shepherd's attic. But then he saw how frightened Aunt Sally was and he remembered how much she mattered to Worzel.

'Please. Do *something*,' Aunt Sally pleaded.

There was a pause. John and Sue exchanged a glance. They had both been wondering how to help Aunt Sally and they'd both had the same idea.

Chapter Three

When Mr Peters got back to the parcels office after his pub lunch, everything still seemed to be in order, so he set about getting the parcels delivered. He had decided that there was so much to go to the Hall he had better get Harry, the farmhand from Scatterbrook, to deliver it all in his horse and cart. Luckily, he'd met Harry in the pub and between them they soon got the cart loaded up with the Colonel's belongings. Harry set off, with the cart piled high, in the direction of the Hall.

Mr Peters decided that he'd deliver the remaining parcel, which was addressed to Mr Shepherd, on foot. It was only a short walk into the village and it would stop Mr Shepherd from turning up at the railway station to complain again. Mr Peters picked up the badly wrapped parcel and walked towards Mr Shepherd's house. He didn't notice that the parcel was a different shape and size from before. After all, the label and packing were the same.

Humming to himself, Mr Peters rang Mr Shepherd's doorbell. Mr Shepherd himself answered the door.

'Package for you, Mr Shepherd,' Mr Peters began. 'Probably that Auntie Alice you've been expecting.'

'Aunt *Sally*,' Mr Shepherd corrected him. The ignorance of some people was amazing, Mr Shepherd thought to himself, as he started to remove the wrapping. 'I hope it's not been damaged,' he said. 'It's a very valuable antique, this Aunt Sally. There's people in the antiques trade who would give their right arms for . . .'

Mr Shepherd broke off. He had finished unwrapping the parcel. It did not contain what he had been waiting for. Inside was the grandmother clock.

'Dangnation take it!' Mr Shepherd exclaimed. 'How many times must you be told? I don't want no grandmother clock, I wants my Aunt Sally!'

Mr Peters gave an embarrassed smile. He was wondering what had happened to the Aunt Sally and how he was going to get it back.

Meanwhile, Harry's horse was pulling its heavy load towards the Hall. Perched on the top of the load in a fine carved chair was Aunt Sally, wooden again, but very pleased with the excellent view of the countryside. She had been lucky that neither Harry nor Mr Peters had known what an Aunt Sally was. They had simply read the label the children had switched round and packed her on to the cart.

The horse turned a corner in the lane and went past a field filled with cows. And Worzel. He'd been chatting to the cows about his Bestest Birthday in an attempt to cheer himself up for the loss of Aunt Sally when the cart went by on the other side of the hedge. Worzel peered over the hedge to see what was going on. His jaw dropped when he saw who was perched on top of the cart.

'Aunt Sally!' he cried, delight written all over his face. 'Why bust my braces, if it ain't Aunt Sally,

given up 'er flighty ways and come back 'ome where she rightly belongs. Back to 'er one an' only true love, ol' Worzel.'

He called over the hedge to her but the cart was already moving along the lane. 'Wait for me, Aunt Sally,' he called. 'It's Worzel!'

Worzel started off after the cart as fast as he could through the field, keeping close to the hedge which stretched alongside the lane. But the cart had a nice clear path to move along and Worzel had to try and push his way through the herd of grazing cows.

'Just slow down a while, me pretty princess,' Worzel called out. 'Your 'andsome prince is on 'is way to –'

At that moment Worzel caught his foot in a rabbit hole and fell full length face down in the field. He soon pulled himself together and got to his feet. But the cart was out of sight. And Worzel was covered from head to foot in mud.

'Dang dratted pesky ol' cows,' Worzel muttered, shaking his fist at them. ''Ow can a body go a-courtin' 'is own true love when I's covered in smelly cow-pat? Reckon I'll have to go an' have a wipe down.' He looked at his filthy front. '*Then* I'll go a-courtin'.' Worzel nipped off across the field to tidy himself. But despite the mess he was in, he was feeling better than he'd felt for days. Aunt Sally had come back to him. And he was going to ask her to marry him. And ask her to come to his Bestest Birthday Party.

Harry the farmhand drove up the long drive to the Hall and delivered the Colonel's belongings to him.

The Colonel made Harry carry everything into the house so Harry expected a good tip. He was disappointed. All he got was five pence and advice to spend it on polish for his shoes. He turned the horse and cart round and drove off back to the village to let everyone know how mean the Colonel was.

The Colonel, however, felt very pleased with himself. Now everything had arrived, he had started to feel that the Hall was really his home. He looked at all the things that Harry had carried into the Hall and memories came back to him of his times in India and Africa. But then his eye fell on an object that had nothing to do with either India or Africa. Indeed he had never seen it before. His fine carved chair was lying on its back and seated on it, with its legs sticking up in the air, was a large wooden doll. Harry must have brought it into the Hall without him noticing.

'I say!' the Colonel exclaimed angrily. 'Someone's playing games. Leaving me with a doll indeed! What would I do with that?' He dashed out and called after Harry, telling him to come back and take the doll away again. But it was no good. Harry was out of earshot. Even if he had noticed the Colonel waving and shouting, he would have been very unlikely to stop after the small tip he'd been given. He didn't even notice Worzel Gummidge, who was standing on the road outside the entrance gates to the Hall, watching the cart go by.

Worzel had tried to clean himself up but he had not been very successful. He still looked very ragged and muddy. But Worzel had more important things to think of now.

'So that's where you've gone to, is it, Aunt Sally?' he said to himself. 'Back to the big 'ouse. Come to your senses and decided to settle down. Not that it makes no difference whether you've come to your senses or is still as barmy as a badger. You's still the only Aunt Sally as'd suit ol' Worzel.'

Looking very determined indeed, Worzel Gummidge went through the gates of the Hall and started the long walk up the drive towards the house itself.

*

Inside the Hall, Colonel Bloodstock was staring crossly at the wooden figure that lay in an untidy heap all across his fine carved chair, wondering what to do with it. He thought the best thing to do was to get in touch with Mr Peters. But a most extraordinary thing happened when he went to tidy the chair up. As he took hold of the front legs of his chair to pull it into the upright position, the wooden figure stopped being a wooden figure and became a very much alive Aunt Sally.

The Colonel blinked in amazement. He'd made a mistake. It wasn't a doll at all but a real live girl! What was she doing in his house?

'Good day, sir,' said Aunt Sally, in her most polite and friendly manner. She realized that this was the Colonel the children had told her about and she wanted to make a good impression.

The Colonel, however, was less than impressed. He told her to be off out of his house and mind her own business. It was at this moment that Aunt Sally had one of her brighter ideas.

'Begging your parding, sir,' she said, giving the Colonel a curtsey. 'This *is* my business. I'm the parlour maid.'

'Parlour maid?' The Colonel was still suspicious. He'd been told the house would be empty and now here was somebody who said she was a servant. 'What were you doing in that chair then?' he asked Aunt Sally.

'Dusting it, sir, begging your parding,' replied Aunt Sally, dropping another curtsey. She was beginning to enjoy herself.

'With your legs in the air?'

'Begging your parding, sir,' Aunt Sally answered, 'but I come over all dizzy and lost my balance and fell in that chair.'

The Colonel stared at Aunt Sally, who smiled back. 'Who took you on as a servant?' he asked.

'I come with the place, sir,' Aunt Sally explained. 'I've always been here.' She was going to add 'ever since I was carved' but luckily stopped herself in time.

Colonel Bloodstock had no idea what to make of this person.

'I'm sure I'll suit,' Aunt Sally continued while he hesitated. 'I'll go an' make you a nice cup of tea, sir, as soon as I've got me proper clothes on.'

Aunt Sally gave another creaky wooden curtsey and went off up the stairs. It was fortunate for her that, after her adventures at the Hall when it was owned by Mrs Bloomsbury-Barton, she knew where things were, including a maid's outfit in one of the wardrobes upstairs.

The Colonel watched her go. 'Odd state of affairs,' he murmured to himself. Still, a cup of tea was a good idea and he didn't see any reason to stop Aunt Sally bringing him one. Then something else took his mind off Aunt Sally altogether. He looked out of one of the front windows and saw a large wood-pigeon sitting amongst his best flowers. The Colonel wasn't fond of birds at the best of times and nothing made him angrier than when they started to ruin his flowers. He snatched up the double-barrelled sporting gun he used when he wanted to scare off birds and rushed out into the grounds at the front of the Hall.

'Be off with you!' the Colonel shouted excitedly. 'Shoo! Shoo!' The pigeon was surprised by this sudden noise and took off into the sky. As it did so, the Colonel fired a shot from the first barrel of his gun. He followed this with a second. The wood-pigeon flew off, thinking to itself that it would have to be more careful in future.

There was someone who was much more frightened of the shots than the pigeon and that was Worzel Gummidge. He was coming up the drive and he nearly jumped out of his straw. When he had calmed down, he watched in amazement as the Colonel stood amongst his best flowers, waving his arms about angrily and shaking his gun. He'd never seen anything like it.

'My oh my, but you're a bad-tempered ol' scarecrow an' no mistake,' Worzel thought as he watched the Colonel. 'Wear yourself out in a week, so you will, scarecrowin' like that when there ain't no crows to scare.'

But Worzel had more important things to think of than the Colonel. He walked round the Hall to the kitchen entrance, where he expected to find his Aunt Sally. Worzel felt quite nervous at meeting her again after so long, especially as he was going to ask her to marry him.

'Now what I needs,' he thought, 'is a nice bunch of flowers to go courtin' with.' He looked round and saw a pot of flowers by the back door that led to the kitchen. It was just right. He picked it up and, leaving the Colonel still shaking his fists at the birds, went into the kitchen to find his Aunt Sally.

Chapter Four

Aunt Sally, now wearing her parlour maid's uniform, was feeling very pleased with her own cleverness. She was not expecting the shock she had when she went into the kitchen. There was Worzel, sitting on a kitchen chair, clutching his pot of flowers and smiling a silly smile.

' 'Ullo, Aunt Sally,' Worzel said brightly.

Aunt Sally decided the best thing to do was to pretend that Worzel wasn't really there. Worzel was the last person she wanted to see now she was living at the Hall. She carried on with making the Colonel's cup of tea.

'I's brought you these flowers, so I 'as,' Worzel continued, holding them out. 'Some on 'em's blue to match your pretty eyes, and others on 'em's red to go with your ruby lips. And I brought 'em so's you know 'ow much I loves you.'

Aunt Sally still said nothing. She filled the kettle with water and ladled spoonful after spoonful of tea from the tea caddy into the pot. Worzel started to get angry at being ignored. He could see Aunt Sally was up to her old tricks.

'If you don't stop pretendin' as if I wasn't 'ere, I'll take this pot o' flowers an' chuck it at your 'ead, so I will,' Worzel said, crossly. 'I knows you can see an' 'ear me!'

Aunt Sally turned to Worzel as if it was the first time she'd noticed him. 'See you? Hear you? *Smell* you, more like.' She looked at his muddy clothes with scorn.

'So would you smell if you'd fallen in a cow-pat afore you come 'ere,' Worzel replied indignantly.

'Disgusting.' Aunt Sally wrinkled her nose and carried on making the tea. This really was too much for Worzel. 'It's disgustin' yourself, Aunt Sally, the way you been behavin'. When I come 'ere this afternoon, in all good faith, I did, ready to forgive an' forget.'

'*You*? Forgive *me*? Hah!' Aunt Sally answered proudly. 'Forgive and forget what, pray?' It really did seem that Aunt Sally had forgotten about the circus and the strong man and Dolly Clothes-Peg. But Worzel knew that Aunt Sally had a habit of forgetting things when it suited her.

'Forget about you bein' as daft as a puddin' an' runnin' away an' joinin' that circus,' Worzel replied.

'It's none of your business,' Aunt Sally snapped, 'what I've been up to.'

'But you're promised to me, Aunt Sally,' Worzel reminded her.

'I'm promised to no one, I'll have you know,' Aunt Sally answered grandly. 'Unless it's the King of Rumania. Or a couple of archdukes.'

'Stop sayin' such things, Aunt Sally,' Worzel said in horror. Worzel didn't know the Hall had a new owner so he had another question to ask. 'If you

ain't promised to me, 'ow come you're back and livin'
'ere with the lady with the big 'at?'

'If you mean Mrs Bloomsbury-Barton,' replied
Aunt Sally, 'I've given 'er the push.'

Worzel gasped. 'You mean you're livin' in this big
'ouse all on your own, Aunt Sally? Why then, ol'
Worzel'll move in with you to protect you.'

'Protect me! Don't be ridiculous!' Aunt Sally exclaimed. 'I'm here in residence with Colonel Bloodstock.'

'Oo's 'e then?' Worzel asked. Then he remembered
the man at the front of the Hall. 'Surely not that 'alf
daft scarecrow outside with a great big shotgun?'

'*Scarecrow?*' Aunt Sally looked very superior.
'Don't be silly. Colonel Bloodstock is an officer and
a gentleman, no less. He's got rows and rows of
medals. Shiny buttons. Beautiful clothes. Reminds me
of the circus, where I come from, so he does.' Aunt
Sally's eyes had that dreamy look in them that
Worzel knew all too well. He felt himself getting
jealous.

'Is just you an' 'im sharin' this big 'ouse, Aunt
Sally?'

'Course we is,' Aunt Sally replied. 'And we get
along famously. Who do you think I've made this
pot of tea for?' she asked, pointing to the tea things.
'And there's more.' She reached into a cupboard and
out of it she took a big chocolate cake.

It looked delicious and Worzel gazed at it longingly. 'Ain't you got a little slice of it for ol' Worzel?'

Aunt Sally looked scornful. She didn't want

37

Worzel around in her new home and she certainly didn't want him to have any cake

'All I've got for you,' she said, 'are a few words of advice. 'Op it before I screams for help, and Colonel Bloodstock rushes in here with his sword and chops you into little pieces and uses them for firewood!'

'You wouldn't do that, Aunt Sally,' Worzel protested. 'Not to Worzel.'

'Wouldn't I just!' Aunt Sally exclaimed grimly. Then she pretended to start screaming. The moment she opened her mouth, Worzel was on his feet. He'd seen enough of the Colonel to know he could be very fierce indeed. Besides, Aunt Sally clearly wasn't going to listen to him.

'I'm off. I can take a 'int,' Worzel said, moving sadly to the kitchen door. 'Worzel knows when 'e ain't wanted. I got my pride, Aunt Sally.'

'Pride!' Aunt Sally scoffed. 'I doubts you know the meaning of the word. You ain't got nothing to be proud of. A military gentleman has got pride. A circus strong man has got pride. But you're nothing but a scaredy-cat scarecrow.'

'You ain't got no call to call me names,' Worzel replied in an upset voice. 'Not when I brung you flowers. They's for you.' He held up the pot of flowers. It was his last hope.

'Thank you, Worzel.' Aunt Sally took the pot of flowers from him. She seemed almost pleased. Perhaps she was fond of him after all, Worzel thought. He left the kitchen and went outside, wondering if his gift might have changed Aunt Sally's mind about him.

He had walked no more than a couple of paces from the kitchen door when something hit him on the back of the head. It was the pot of flowers. Aunt Sally had thrown it, and thrown it so hard she had knocked Worzel's Bestest Head sideways. Worzel was too shocked and upset to do anything in return.

'You see,' Aunt Sally cried, smiling grimly, 'you're just what I said, a cowardy custard scarecrow!' And before Worzel could reply, she went back inside, slamming the door behind her.

Worzel straightened his Bestest Head sadly. It hurt him that Aunt Sally said he was a coward without any pride. Especially when he'd come all the way up to the Hall to see her. 'I'll show you who's a coward, Aunt Sally,' he muttered to himself. 'I'll go an' give that mad man with the gun a tellin' off. You just see if I don't.'

Worzel walked round to the front of the Hall to show Aunt Sally he was braver than the Colonel, whatever she might say. 'I ain't afraid o' nobody nor nothin'!' Worzel boasted to himself. He thought for a moment. 'Except maybe rats an' creepy-crawly spiders an' b–b–b . . . them things what smoke comes out of.'

Worzel was so frightened of bonfires and what they could do to scarecrows that he could never bear to say the word 'bonfire'. This time he was saved from having to say anything more at all because he heard a shot from the Colonel's shotgun. Worzel nearly jumped out of his skin again. The shot made him forget everything else he was afraid of. He had to remind himself that he was supposed to prove he was brave to Aunt Sally. He pulled himself together and walked on towards the Colonel.

Colonel Bloodstock was still busy trying to frighten away the wood-pigeon. He hadn't yet succeeded so he was getting very cross. He gazed in astonishment when he saw Worzel coming towards him.

'What are you doing on my land?' the Colonel asked in a fierce voice. 'Might I ask what you think you're at?'

Worzel felt himself trembling but did his best to look bold. He stared back into the Colonel's angry red face and took a deep breath. 'It's me as wants to know what you're at,' he began. 'Livin' 'ere with an Aunt Sally as is promised to someone else. And why are you standin' out 'ere shootin' at that ol' wood-pigeon so as to take the chocklit cake out of some 'onest scarecrow's mouth?'

'Scarecrow?' roared Colonel Bloodstock. 'Are you calling me a scarecrow?'

Worzel nodded. 'What's wrong with bein' a scarecrow may I ask?'

The Colonel had no idea what Worzel was talking about. 'You're the one that looks like a scarecrow,' he replied. 'Look at the filthy mess you're in. Be off with you. Go on, clear off.'

Colonel Bloodstock looked so fierce that Worzel's first thought was to run away. But he remembered he had to be brave. He stood up straight and took a big swallow. 'Shan't. Ain't goin' away nowheres. Not till I get a polite answer from you.'

The Colonel was not used to being talked to like this. Here was a dirty tramp standing on *his* land and refusing to move. Just the sort of man who would have been better and tidier if he had been a soldier under the Colonel when he was fighting one of his wars. 'Look at you,' the Colonel said. 'What a shower! A few years as a soldier would make a man of you.' He paused, imagining Worzel in battle. 'I'd like to see how you'd stand up under fire.'

It was the worst thing the Colonel could have said. To the Colonel fire meant guns in battle, but to Worzel fire meant only one thing. Bonfire. All his courage left him at once.

'Don't mention that word, please, your honour,' Worzel pleaded.

The Colonel saw he was shaking. 'Go on. Clear off,' he ordered, 'before I shoot this gun at you.' He shook it in Worzel's face. 'And just remember, I'm an expert shot. I never miss. Look at that lot!'

The Colonel pointed back through the window into the drawing room. For the first time, Worzel saw all the stuffed animal heads that the Colonel had been unpacking from his luggage. Worzel was horrified.

'There's plenty of room for one more,' the Colonel growled.

Worzel gulped. He had a sudden picture in his mind of his own Bestest Head hung up on a wall between the heads of two fierce animals. The Colonel fired a shot into the air as a warning. Worzel started to back away.

'Sorry to be such a bother, sir, beggin' your parding. Good day to 'ee, sir!' Worzel said, in his politest voice. Then, as soon as he had finished his apologies, he turned and ran away as fast as his straw legs would carry him.

'Good riddance,' the Colonel called out. 'Don't let me find you on my land again, do you hear?'

Worzel ran for dear life down the drive to the gates. He could just make out what the Colonel was shouting after him. He was saying that Worzel was a coward. And he was shouting it so loudly that no doubt Aunt Sally would hear what he was saying. Coward. The word echoed in Worzel's head. Was Aunt Sally right? Was he nothing but a coward? And what could he do about it?

One thing was certain. Unless he proved to Aunt Sally that he was brave, he would never be able to invite her to his Bestest Birthday Party.

Chapter Five

The Crowman was surprised when Worzel came to visit him at his house. Worzel had been very quiet since the Crowman had brought him back from the fairground. But the Crowman knew that with Worzel there was always trouble sooner or later. He was more surprised when Worzel explained that he wanted a new head. A brave head.

'You want a brave head, do you, Worzel?' the Crowman asked.

Worzel nodded. 'If it's all the same to you, your exuberance.'

The Crowman looked grave. 'But it isn't all the same to me, Worzel. Nor would it be all the same to you. Bravery's not something you put on or take off like a hat. It's either there or it isn't. And it comes from the heart, not the head.'

'I ain't got a 'eart, your eminence,' Worzel replied, touching his straw chest. He couldn't understand why, if he could have a counting head to help him to count and a reading head to help him to read, he couldn't have a brave head to make him brave and impress Aunt Sally. He touched his chest again. 'But I feels things' inside 'ere, your magickness.'

'Not of my making, Worzel,' the Crowman replied.

'I know that,' Worzel said. 'But they're in there all

45

the same. Feelin's for Aunt Sally. Bigger than if I 'ad a 'eart even. Feels as if these feelin's fills up my whole body.'

The Crowman shook his head slowly. Whenever he wanted to get cross with Worzel, he always remembered how many of Worzel's troubles came about because he was so fond of Aunt Sally. The Crowman found himself being kinder than he meant to be. He spoke more gently. 'If you feel that strongly about Aunt Sally, Worzel, you don't need a head from me to make you do what's best for both of you.'

Worzel was not to be put off that easily. 'Begging your parding, Mr Crowman, sir, but all you gave me for a 'ead was a turnip. What chance do a turnip-'eaded scarecrow stand against a circus strong man with shiny black 'air? Or a military gentleman with a load o' medals?'

'And you think a brave head on your shoulders would make all the difference, do you?' asked the Crowman.

'Only if your 'ighness pleases,' Worzel replied humbly.

The Crowman thought for a moment. 'There *is* such a head, Worzel,' he began, slowly. 'Though it hasn't seen the light of day for over sixty years.' He moved over to a cupboard stuck away in one of the darkest corners of the room and took out a dusty box. It was the sort of box you might keep an old military drum in. The Crowman hesitated before opening it. 'I'm not sure even now that it wouldn't be better to leave it rest another sixty years.'

'Mightn't we just take a peek at it, your kind-
liness?' Worzel asked, staring eagerly at the box.

But before doing anything else, the Crowman
wanted to explain to Worzel that the head in the box
belonged to a scarecrow long gone, who had stood in
the middle of a battlefield in a long, hard-fought war
many many years ago. When he pulled it out, Worzel
gasped. It was the head of no ordinary scarecrow
but of a fierce warlike soldier. It had a big, stiff,
spiked moustache, a scar running along one cheek
made by a sword cut, and on its head a spiked metal

47

helmet of the kind that was worn in battles many years ago.

'That's a fearful scary 'ead,' Worzel muttered.

'It belonged to a scarecrow that never moved one inch from its post while cannons fired to its right and its left. Huge armies fought around it but it stood its place.' The Crowman paused impressively. 'This head, Worzel, is the bravest scarecrow head that ever drew breath.'

Worzel stared in wonder. 'If only I 'ad a 'ead like that, Mr Crowman, sir,' he said, 'I could sweep Aunt Sally right off her pretty little feet, so I could.'

The Crowman shook his head again. 'If only all of us were something we are not. But, alas, we're all just as our particular maker chose to make us.'

But Worzel wasn't listening. 'May I try it on, just the once?' he asked eagerly, nodding at the head as the Crowman held it in his hands.

'Worzel,' the Crowman replied, 'Can't you get it into your head – the one you've got on – that this head was never meant for you?'

But Worzel's Bestest Head was too full of thoughts of impressing Aunt Sally to understand what the Crowman was saying. 'I don't want to keep it, your goodliness,' he explained. 'Only to borrow it.'

The Crowman sighed and put the head back in its drum-shaped box. 'I showed you this head, Worzel, because I hoped it might inspire you to be brave in your own right. I never meant that you should wear it.'

Worzel was disappointed. The Crowman had

given him hundreds of different heads in the past to do different things, all of them cowardly. He was just asking for *one* that was brave. He started to protest.

'Enough!' The Crowman's strong voice cut him off and the Crowman's strong eyes looked at him closely. 'I am the Crowman, Worzel. I have said what is to be said. And if you don't have the courage to do what needs to be done on your own then get back to Ten-acre Field at once. Before I lose my patience and give your job to another scarecrow.'

'Yes, your majestickness.' Worzel knew it was useless to argue. The Crowman had made him and the Crowman could unmake him. It was as simple as that.

*

The rest of the day, Worzel could think of nothing but getting the brave head. All thoughts of his birthday were gone. John and Sue couldn't find him when they went to play in the barn. Worzel was away on his own, wandering about with the words of Aunt Sally calling him a coward ringing in his ears.

In the end, Worzel decided, there was only one thing to do. If the Crowman wouldn't give him the head, he would have to steal it. The thought of stealing from the Crowman made Worzel shake all over but there seemed to be nothing else for it.

That night, a shadowy figure could be seen tiptoeing across the Crowman's garden after the Crowman was tucked up in bed and asleep. It was Worzel. When he got to the door of the Crowman's house, he could hear the Crowman snoring and that gave him courage to open the door and creep in. Luckily, there were no curtains on the window and the moonlight streamed in. Otherwise, Worzel would never have been able to find his way around. As it was, he had a bad time of it. A floorboard creaked when he put his foot on it, and when he backed away in fright he nearly knocked a vase off a table and only caught it at the last moment before it crashed to the floor. However, the Crowman seemed to sleep on, and, after several long pauses to get his courage together, Worzel made his way across to the cupboard where the Crowman kept the brave head in its box.

Once it was in his hands, Worzel moved as quickly as he could across the floor and back through the door. Here he nearly tripped as he backed out of the house but just stopped himself in time. A few moments later, he was off across the garden and down the road with the precious box in his hands.

If Worzel had stayed a little longer in the room, he would have had a surprise. No sooner had he shut the door than the Crowman sat up in bed wide awake. He had heard everything and it worried him. He sighed.

'Oh Worzel, Worzel! I hoped the head might have given you a little courage of your own. All it's given you is the courage to *steal* the head.' He sighed again.

'So be it,' the Crowman said. 'Learn for yourself. And remember, Worzel, if you must wear that head, wear it well. It's something to be proud of.'

Chapter Six

Just after dawn the next day, a most unusual sight was to be seen in the country lane that led to the Hall. It was Worzel riding along on top of the elderly horse that belonged to the milkman. The horse was rather enjoying this early morning adventure but could not manage more than a slow walking pace because of its age. Not that this worried Worzel, who felt proud and brave. This wasn't surprising, because he was now wearing the brave head he had taken from the Crowman.

It was odd to see Worzel wearing a fierce military head with stiff moustaches and a spiked helmet. Particularly as he had added to his costume a tattered cloak tied over his shoulders, a battered bugle hung round his neck and a long pointed stick to use as a lance if anyone attacked him. Worzel looked less like a soldier of sixty years ago than a knight in armour of four hundred years ago. But either way he didn't look much like the cowardly Worzel that everybody knew.

Worzel rode up to the gates of the Hall and up the drive. He tried to persuade the horse to go a bit faster and the horse did its best. When he was just outside the Hall itself, Worzel told the horse to stop. He put the bugle to his lips and blew with all his might. The bugle made a loud trumpet-like sound,

not very musical but loud enough to wake people up. Which was what Worzel wanted. He blew the bugle again.

A window on the first floor of the house opened and a figure dressed in pyjamas peered out. It was Colonel Bloodstock, woken by the bugle. He could not believe his eyes when he saw Worzel and the horse standing there.

Another window on the first floor of the house opened almost immediately afterwards. This time it was Aunt Sally who looked out, dressed in her nightgown. She behaved rather differently from the Colonel. She thought Worzel looked so brave and splendid that it made her proud to see him. 'Oh, Worzel, Worzel!' she called in delight.

Her cry encouraged Worzel. 'Give me back the girl I love,' he called to the Colonel in a loud, strong voice. 'Or come down here and fight me for 'er.'

Worzel was almost as astonished as the Colonel at how brave and strong he felt with his new head on. He wasn't in the least scared when the Colonel started threatening him with all sorts of terrible punishments if he didn't get off the Colonel's land. Instead, Worzel took off one of his tattered gloves and, after waving it at the Colonel, threw it down on the grass.

'Look,' he called, 'I've thrown down my glove. That means I challenges you to a duel.' He stared boldly at the Colonel.

Colonel Bloodstock thought he must be dealing with a madman. He thought about calling the police to get rid of him, but then decided he could take care of things himself. After all, it was *his* home and he wasn't going to let anybody scare him out of it. He shut his window, pulled on his trousers over his pyjamas and snatched up his sporting gun. He rushed downstairs to the front door, where he collided with Aunt Sally, who had also run downstairs, having quickly pulled on her ordinary clothes. Aunt Sally was very excited about the whole thing. Two brave men were going to fight for her love. It was what she had always imagined should happen.

'Keep well behind me, girl,' Colonel Bloodstock ordered Aunt Sally, as he came out of the front door. 'It's an officer's duty to protect the women and children, you know. And that fellow's nuttier than a fruitcake.'

The Colonel came out cautiously, holding his gun at the ready. Aunt Sally followed, but the Colonel told her to stay near the front door while he went to deal with Worzel.

Worzel watched him come nearer. 'Get off my land,' the Colonel shouted. 'I'm warning you. This is your last chance.'

Normally the sight of the gun would have been enough to frighten Worzel. But now he felt no fear at all. Instead, he raised the long lance he had in his hand and shouted back to the Colonel: 'Prepare to die, you coward!' Then Worzel lowered the lance so that it stuck straight out in front of him at about the height of the Colonel's head, put his bugle to his lips and ordered the horse to gallop forward.

'Chaa . . . arge!'

The Colonel raised his sporting gun to his shoulder as he saw Worzel coming nearer. 'I'm warning you,' he shouted back. 'If you don't stop, I'll fire both barrels at you.'

As the Colonel took aim, Worzel galloped towards him. Aunt Sally watched them both in rapture. Then the Colonel fired. There was a huge bang and both of the barrels let off shots at the same time. They hit Worzel full in the chest. But, of course, Worzel was made of straw. They went straight through him and out the other side without harming him at all. Worzel galloped on.

This was too much for Colonel Bloodstock. He was no coward, but he'd never seen two shots go straight through somebody like that before. He began to think he was up against something very strange and dangerous indeed. In fact, he started to panic. As Worzel galloped closer, he turned and ran away, looking for cover in the Hall. Unfortunately, he didn't look where he was going because he was in such a panic. He crashed straight through a greenhouse and disappeared from sight.

'Oh, Worzel! My hero!' Aunt Sally stood on the steps of the Hall, her eyes filled with wonder and admiration. She had never seen Worzel like this before. Worzel, his brave head still filled with pride, galloped up to where she stood, leaned down and easily lifted Aunt Sally up. He swung her on to the saddle beside him and they rode off on the horse, which by now was thoroughly enjoying the whole

adventure. For Aunt Sally, it was like all her dreams come true. Her brave knight had rescued her and was going to carry her off. Worzel was happy too. Except for one thing. He was wondering what would happen when he had to take his brave head off again.

Dreams don't last for ever. And Aunt Sally's lasted less than most. She had expected to be carried off into the sunset as everyone is in romantic stories. Instead, she was taken back to Worzel's barn where John's swing was. And Worzel had to return the horse to the milkman before he missed him when he started his milk round. And, worst of all, Worzel took off the brave head, stuffed it back in its drum-shaped box and put his ordinary head on. Aunt Sally felt her disappointment grow every minute. She began to regret leaving Colonel Bloodstock and the Hall.

'I wanted to be carried off into a glowing sunset,' she complained to Worzel, 'not carried off into a filthy barn.'

'You knows I couldn't do that, Aunt Sally,' Worzel replied, 'owin' to the fact that I 'ad to get the 'orse back to the milkman afore breakfast time. But we can be 'appy 'ere together, you an' me, just the two of us. Can't we?' He looked hopefully at his beloved Aunt Sally, but somehow he knew that things hadn't changed. Aunt Sally still wouldn't be happy just to be with him and live together for ever.

'Happy? *Here*?' Aunt Sally sniffed. 'It smells like a cowshed!'

'No, it don't, Aunt Sally,' Worzel replied. 'It

58

smells like a pig-sty. That's because it's next to the pig-sty, see? But it don't smell like a cowshed, not at all.' He pulled back his cloak and showed his mud-stained clothes. 'It's me as smells like a cowshed.'

The sight was too much for Aunt Sally. She burst into tears. 'You're hopeless,' she cried. 'I'm worse off than I was before. I've never been so unhappy in my whole life!'

She ran out of the barn in tears. Worzel, still carrying the box with the head in it, followed after her. 'But Aunt Sally,' he shouted. 'I's your 'ero.'

Aunt Sally wasn't listening. She ran across the farmyard and disappeared out of sight. Worzel knew there was no point in trying to follow her. It was like when she ran off to join the travelling fair all over again. He hadn't even had time to tell her about his Bestest Birthday Party. He stood still by the door of the barn.

'I'll take charge of that box, Worzel, if you please.'

It was the Crowman, who'd entered the farmyard without Worzel seeing him. His voice made Worzel jump.

'Oh, sorry, your 'oliness. I didn't see you there!'

The Crowman held out his hand and Worzel passed him the box. Worzel was so sad and gloomy that the Crowman didn't have the heart to tell him off.

'From what I've heard, Worzel,' he said in a not unkind voice, 'you did the head no disgrace. You wore it well.'

Worzel nodded, a touch of pride coming back into

his face. 'That I did, your magnificence. I was 'er 'ero, Mr Crowman. I was 'er brave fighter. I rescued 'er.'

'Yes, Worzel,' the Crowman replied gently. 'But bravery doesn't bring happiness, does it?'

'It brought me 'appiness, your worship,' Worzel replied, remembering how he'd frightened the Colonel and lifted Aunt Sally on to his horse.

'Happiness for a few moments, maybe, Worzel,' the Crowman continued. 'But there's many brave actions that have ended as no more than a tear in a woman's eye.'

'Don't seem right and fair some'ow,' Worzel said sadly, 'after all I done for Aunt Sally.'

The Crowman walked away towards his tricycle, carrying the drum-shaped box. 'Bravery,' he said, as he climbed on his tricycle, 'has made fools of wiser men than you, Worzel.' He cycled off out of the farmyard. Tears filled Worzel's eyes. After all he'd hoped, Aunt Sally was gone again. And without her, there could be no proper birthday. But perhaps she wouldn't get so far this time. Perhaps she'd turn up again. Perhaps she'd turn up on his Bestest Birthday and say she loved him. Worzel started to dry his tears. Where Aunt Sally was concerned, he could never give up hope for too long.

Chapter Seven

Later that morning, John and Sue were sitting in the caravan in which they lived with their father. They were playing a board game, but their minds weren't really on it. They were thinking about Worzel.

'I don't see why we should give him a present,' John said.

'*Why* not?' Sue replied.

'Well, he wouldn't give us a present if it was our birthday. And we only have one every year. He's always having them.'

'But this one's his *best* birthday,' answered Sue. 'We ought to give him something.'

John didn't look so sure. 'We don't even know when it is.'

'Worzel said we'd find out.' As usual, Sue took a much brighter view of Worzel than her brother. 'He said one day we'd go into that field, and we'd see something rare enough to make our stummicks tickle.'

John grunted. 'Anyway, I don't expect we'll be hearing anything more about the birthday *now*. Not with Aunt Sally back.'

'Yes, I wonder what's happened,' Sue said thoughtfully. They'd heard and seen nothing of either Worzel or Aunt Sally since they'd saved Aunt

Sally from a return to Mr Shepherd's attic, and Sue feared they might both be in trouble.

'But anyway, whatever happens,' Sue decided, 'I still think we should get Worzel something. He has asked us to his party, after all.'

John was unimpressed. 'Who cares?'

'Nobody.' The voice was Worzel's and it sounded very sad. They looked up and saw Worzel peering through the open window of the caravan. Sue wanted to invite him in but John pointed out that their father might come back and find him there. Instead, they went off to the barn, where Worzel told them all his troubles. Even John felt sorry for him when he heard what had happened about Aunt Sally.

'I'm sure she'll turn up again, Worzel,' he said.

'Oh yes,' Sue added. 'She can't get very far from the village on her own.'

The children both hoped Worzel hadn't heard them arguing about his birthday present. But he had other things on his mind. He was starting to feel sad and lonely again.

*

In fact, the children were right. Aunt Sally was so angry and upset with Worzel that, without thinking, she ran straight for the village. And the first person she saw was Mr Shepherd. She hardly had time to make herself all wooden again before he found her.

Mr Shepherd was very puzzled to discover his long lost Aunt Sally in the middle of the road. But he decided whoever had stolen it from the railway station had changed their mind about taking it and left it there in the street. He picked up the Aunt Sally as best he could and carried her into the village.

But Mr Shepherd didn't carry her back home. The reason Mr Shepherd wanted his figure so badly was not to keep it at home. It was because he had thought of a very good use for it. A use he hoped would be very profitable.

In the middle of the village High Street was a smart tea shop. It was run by a thin middle-aged lady called Miss Maple. She had only recently taken over the shop and wanted to attract lots of new customers. Mr Shepherd called on her and explained about the Aunt Sally. He suggested it would be a great attraction. Miss Maple could put a large menu board in the figure's hand, listing all the things to eat in the shop, then everyone going by would notice.

Miss Maple liked the idea so much that she wanted to buy the Aunt Sally there and then. But Mr Shepherd had other ideas. First of all he offered to set the Aunt Sally up outside, with the menu board in its hand. 'Just to see if it'll work, Miss Maple,' he explained.

When he'd done that, he came back into the tea shop and told Miss Maple how good it looked. Again she offered to buy the figure off him. Mr Shepherd shook his head.

'You wait till you've seen how it works, Miss Maple. It's a valuable antique. Been all over the country – fairs and fêtes and so forth. But I'll be happy to lend it to you for as long as you like. Just so long as you don't mind me popping by for a cup of tea occasionally. Just to keep an eye on the Aunt Sally.'

This was so reasonable that Miss Maple agreed. Mr Shepherd decided to make immediate use of his bargain and seated himself at a table. He asked for some cake and a cup of tea. Miss Maple got the waitress to serve him with them. It was only when Miss Maple saw how greedily Mr Shepherd helped himself to her cakes that she began to wonder whether she had made the best bargain after all. Still, she would wait and see if the Aunt Sally brought her more customers.

The Aunt Sally stood outside the tea shop with the menu board in its hand the rest of the morning and into the afternoon. Luckily Aunt Sally was still wooden, so she didn't feel how undignified her position was.

It was during that afternoon that Worzel Gummidge decided to cheer himself up by coming into the village and looking in at the tea shop.

He was, of course, delighted when he saw Aunt Sally standing outside. He could hardly believe his luck at finding her so soon. He went up to look closer at the menu she was holding in her stiff wooden hand. Worzel's reading was so bad that he peered at the menu without having the least idea what it said. But Worzel was ever hopeful. 'Maybe it's a note saying she's sorry and that she'll marry me after all,' he said quietly to himself.

'It don't say no such thing.' Aunt Sally came back to life with a start.

'I wondered how long you was going to go on sulking,' Worzel replied. He knew better than to talk about Colonel Bloodstock or the brave head. Aunt Sally had a very short memory and it was even shorter when it came to things she didn't like. Instead, he pointed to the menu.

'What *does* it say then?' he asked.

'It's a menu.'

'Oh, arr,' Worzel said, none the wiser. 'What's a menu, Aunt Sally? An' why are you standin' out 'ere 'oldin' it?'

'A menu tells you what they've got to eat in there,' Aunt Sally replied, sniffily. 'I was wondering whether to pop in for a snack.' She didn't like to tell Worzel the truth.

'I'll come in with you, if you like, Aunt Sally,' said Worzel, his eyes lighting up. 'I could just manage a cup o' tea an' a slice o' cake.'

Aunt Sally looked disapproving. 'I should think *I* should require something a bit more grand than that! The very idea of being seen out dining with a common scarecrow completely puts me off my appetite, anyway.'

All signs of admiration for Worzel which Aunt Sally had shown when he'd rescued her were gone. But Worzel was not to be put off that easily now he'd found his Aunt Sally yet again. 'I'll tell you a secret if you likes, Aunt Sally,' he began, speaking close to her ear, 'as'll bring you your appetite back, I reckon.'

'What's that?'

'I'll give you a 'int,' Worzel answered slyly. 'Just three little words. *Birthday cake.*'

'What birthday cake?' Aunt Sally asked suspiciously.

'It's going to be my Bestest Birthday soon, for this 'ere 'ead,' Worzel said proudly. 'You can come to my party if you wants.'

Aunt Sally wrinkled her nose. 'Me? Attend a party for a smelly scarecrow's 'ead? I wouldn't be seen dead at such a thing.'

'You wouldn't want to go there dead, Aunt Sally,' Worzel replied. ' 'Cos if you was dead, you wouldn't be able to eat up all the eatables there's going to be.'

'What kind of eatables?' Aunt Sally asked, beginning to be a bit more interested.

Worzel thought quickly. 'Oh, some nice 'taters and some of the apples that got left over from last year and, oo knows, when ol' Farmer Braithwaite's back is turned I might be able to pinch a bucket o' pigswill before the pigs get to eat it.'

'*Pigswill!*' Aunt Sally shrieked. She had listened to this list with growing disgust, but that was too much. It made her furious to think anyone could offer someone as grand as herself such terrible food. It made her so furious that she hit Worzel over the head with the heavy wooden menu board. And she followed that by hitting him in the stomach with it too. Worzel gave a grunt and grabbed at the menu, but Aunt Sally was too cross to bother about that. She started off down the High Street, still furious, leaving Worzel, stunned by her blows, holding on to the menu.

It was just at this moment that Mr Shepherd came out of the tea shop, followed by Miss Maple. Worzel barely had time to make himself stiff and lifeless. Mr Shepherd, filled with tea and cakes as his part of the bargain, was boasting to Miss Maple about the beauty of his Aunt Sally. He pointed to where Worzel now stood, holding the menu.

He broke off in horror. Miss Maple was horrified too.

'That ain't my Aunt Sally!' Mr Shepherd cried.

'I don't care what it is,' Miss Maple replied. 'Get rid of it. That won't attract new customers. It'll frighten them away.'

She turned and went back into the tea shop, leaving Mr Shepherd gazing open-mouthed at the scarecrow. He didn't know that Worzel was wondering the same thing as him. Where had Aunt Sally gone?

Chapter Eight

Aunt Sally with her clumsy wooden walk didn't get far. Mr Shepherd found her, stiff and wooden, close to the place he'd discovered her before. He carried her back to the tea shop. Worzel, meanwhile, made use of the confusion to sneak away and hide. He watched as Mr Shepherd put the menu back in Aunt Sally's hand and went back into the shop to tell Miss Maple the figure had been found. But Worzel knew there was no point in trying to talk to Aunt Sally about his birthday party again just yet. All he'd get was another hard knock over the head with the menu board.

Instead he went back to the barn and told John and Sue his troubles.

'Well, I think it's mean of Aunt Sally to turn down your invitation, Worzel,' Sue said. John agreed with her.

Worzel sighed. 'On the other 'and,' he said gloomily, 'you can understand 'er feelings, see. What 'ave I got to offer 'er? A grand lady of 'er breedin'? Apples an' taters an' nuts an' pigswill. Well, it ain't what she's used to, is it? She dines with duchesses and archdooks, my Aunt Sally does. She's told me so 'erself. So what call would she 'ave to go to ol' Worzel's birthday party? Even if it is 'is Bestest one?'

The children could see that in a way it was worse for Worzel now Aunt Sally was in the village and wouldn't come than if she'd been miles and miles away and *couldn't* come.

'I wouldn't let her spoil *my* birthday, Worzel,' Sue said.

'I could kick 'er up an' down the 'Igh Street so I could,' Worzel said. 'But it won't do no good, will it? No matter 'ow 'ard I kicks 'er. 'Cos she's got a stubborn streak in 'er, which comes from bein' 'igh born.' He looked gloomier still. 'If I can't 'ave 'er there, I shan't 'ave no birthday party. I shall just sit 'ere and sulk.'

And, as the children watched, Worzel's face started to freeze into a sulk. The children knew what that meant. He could hold his stiff sulky position for days and days. John sighed. He looked at Sue. If Worzel was going to sulk, they'd *have* to do something about his birthday.

It was late afternoon when the children arrived outside the tea shop and peered in. The shop was full, so perhaps Aunt Sally was getting Miss Maple some new customers. At one table the children could see Mr Shepherd explaining to Miss Maple his ideas about who had tried to steal the Aunt Sally. Miss Maple listened with a stony face because, as he spoke, Mr Shepherd was eating large numbers of cakes and eclairs, washed down with tea, and, by their bargain, not paying a penny for his feast.

At a table nearby, Mr and Mrs Braithwaite were also having tea. They were not too pleased with the weak tea they'd been served, nothing like the rich brew they had at home. And at another table Colonel Bloodstock, his face bandaged, was telling whoever would listen about his extraordinary adventure with an escaped lunatic on a horse, who had stolen his maid away. Not, the Colonel admitted, that he missed *her* very much.

But it wasn't the people inside who caught the children's eyes. It was the window of the shop, filled with delicious-looking cakes and pastries. In the centre of it was a large birthday cake covered in icing.

It was one of the best birthday cakes the children had ever seen. Sue made up her mind immediately. They would buy the cake and give Worzel a surprise party.

'It would be the best present Worzel could possibly have,' she said to John. John was less sure. 'We can't pay for a whole birthday party, Sue. You know that. We haven't got enough money.'

'We wouldn't need to pay for everything,' Sue replied, thinking out loud. 'We could ask Mrs Braithwaite to make us some sandwiches. We could say it was for a picnic.'

'She might give us some apple pie as well,' John put in, getting enthusiastic in spite of himself. '*And* we could ask Dad to bring us some packets of crisps every time he goes to the pub. Different flavours. You know, Smoky Bacon, Cheese and Onion, Salt and Vinegar. And we've got two full bottles of lemonade in the caravan.'

'Exactly,' Sue replied. 'All we'd need to *buy* would be the birthday cake.' They both looked again at the magnificent cake in the window.

'How much do you think a cake like that costs?' John asked.

Sue shrugged. 'Well, I've got three weeks' pocket money saved up.'

'And Harry still owes me money for helping him clean out the pig-sties last week,' John replied.

'And then there's what we've got in our money boxes,' Sue added. 'I bet we *could* afford it, John.'

John nodded. He was all in favour of the idea now.

'It'd be the Bestest Birthday Party Worzel ever had.'

They both knew that someone had been listening to every word they said. Although she was still wooden, Aunt Sally was very close by. But it was only now that Sue glanced across at the Aunt Sally figure and said in a very loud disapproving voice, '*Someone* might wish she'd never said she wouldn't come to Worzel's party.'

They left Aunt Sally to think about that and went back home to the caravan.

*

That night the children both found it difficult to sleep. They were turning over the party plans in their heads and wanted to discuss them with each other. They wanted to be sure that Worzel didn't find out about the treat they were planning for him. He'd not been in the barn when they'd got back, so they hoped he'd gone back to his post in Ten-acre Field.

They still had one big worry. 'We don't know which day Worzel's birthday is to be, do we?' John said.

'He said we'd find out, didn't he?' Sue answered. 'We'll know when it is, don't you worry.'

The next morning Sue walked across the fields as soon as it was light. Her head was full of the birthday plans and she wanted to take a look at the empty meadow Worzel had shown them before all the adventures with the return of Aunt Sally. She had visited it several times without seeing any change at

all and was still puzzled by what Worzel had meant.

She opened the gate and walked into the meadow. A surprise awaited her. Overnight, the empty meadow had blossomed into a mass of richly coloured wild flowers. They spread everywhere, almost burying the green grass. The sight was so beautiful that it took Sue's breath away. She stood still, slowly taking in the variety of colours. Then suddenly she felt a tickling in her stomach.

It was only then that Sue realized. This was the feeling Worzel had said she would get. This was the sign he'd talked about.

'It's today! It's today!' she shouted.

She started to run back to tell John, calling out as she went, in her excitement: 'Today! It's today! It's Worzel's Bestest Birthday!'

Chapter Nine

John was as excited as Sue when she told him about the Bestest Birthday. But they knew they would have to move very fast now if they were going to be able to give Worzel the surprise party they'd planned. Sue emptied their piggy banks with the aid of a knife, while John ran to collect the money he was owed for helping Harry the farmhand. Harry paid up reluctantly. Then they talked to Mrs Braithwaite about going on a picnic that day and, as luck would have it, she was doing a special bake that day. They got not only sandwiches but also fresh buns and jam tarts in large numbers. And after lunch Mr Peters came back from the pub with a good supply of crisps and cheese biscuits, as they'd asked him to. He wondered why they were suddenly wanting so many, but the children didn't bother to try and explain. They were too busy.

It was early afternoon before John and Sue had got everything together and could go down to the village with the money they'd collected to buy Worzel's birthday cake at the tea shop. It was a proud moment when Miss Maple handed over the cake, beautifully wrapped, inside a cardboard box.

'Carry it carefully now,' she said. The children nodded. They were so excited that they didn't notice the Crowman taking his tea quietly at a table in the corner of the shop. But the Crowman noticed them. His sharp eyes saw what they had bought and his sharp mind made a good guess as to who it was for.

The children came out of the shop with Sue carefully carrying the cake. They walked straight past Aunt Sally, who stood outside with the wooden menu, pretending not to see her. But of course Aunt Sally saw them, and it made her very anxious. The sight of the birthday cake disappearing from the window had made her very curious, and now she saw it in Sue's hands she began to regret what she had said to Worzel.

While Aunt Sally was wondering what to do, an elderly gentleman came up to have a look at the menu. His eyesight was poor, and in order to see it better he took hold of the menu. Aunt Sally was still wooden but was getting more and more anxious as she saw the children disappearing up the High Street. She felt herself getting hungrier and hungrier. In the end she could stand it no longer. Ignoring the trouble it might get her into, she rushed after the children, leaving the elderly gentleman holding the menu.

When he looked up from his reading the old gentleman had a shock. The figure he thought had been holding the menu had disappeared. He began to wonder if his eyesight was getting worse than ever.

Meanwhile, Aunt Sally had caught the children up. They knew why she was there but didn't want to be too friendly because of the way she had treated Worzel. As they walked, Aunt Sally gazed greedily at the cake in its box. She offered to carry it but the children didn't trust her not to eat it there and then.

When they got back to Scatterbrook Farm, John ran off to fetch Worzel from Ten-acre Field, where he was supposed to be scaring the crows. Sue and Aunt Sally went into the barn, where Sue started to put up paperchains and balloons to make it look more birthday-like. The children had already put out a makeshift table, which they'd covered with plates of crisps, buns, jam tarts and sandwiches. The cake was placed in the centre of the table. Aunt Sally took it all in greedily but pretended to be too proud to be bothered with all this food. Sue, however, knew she had to keep a sharp look out while she worked, in case Aunt Sally began stealing the food before Worzel arrived.

When she'd finished decorating the barn, Sue stood back to admire her work. 'How's that?' she asked Aunt Sally.

'Quite nice for what it is, I suppose,' Aunt Sally replied grandly. 'Not what I'm used to, of course, but good enough considering it's just a scarecrow's birthday party.'

'But it isn't *just* a scarecrow,' Sue protested. 'It's Worzel. And it isn't *just* his birthday either. It's his bestest one.'

Aunt Sally looked very bored and turned towards the table. 'While we're waiting for him, wouldn't it be a good idea to cut the cake?'

'What for?' Sue asked.

'Because that's what you're supposed to do in the best circles,' Aunt Sally answered proudly. 'You do it to make sure the cake ain't gone off. Cakes do, you know. We could cut it up into three bits. You could eat one bit and I could eat two bits.' She paused. 'And when Worzel gets here, he could eat the other bits.'

'No,' Sue said firmly.

'Then how about a party game? To pass the time.' Aunt Sally suggested. 'We could play "hunt the birthday cake",' she continued, moving hungrily towards the cake. 'To start the game off, I'll take the cake outside and –'

'No!' said Sue, even more firmly. 'We're not touching anything until John comes back with Worzel.' Aunt Sally returned sulkily to where she had been sitting.

Sue heard footsteps. 'It must be John and Worzel!' She turned to Aunt Sally. 'Come on, join in singing.' And Sue started to sing, 'Happy birthday to you, happy birthday to you, happy bir –'

Sue stopped. John had entered alone. There was no Worzel with him. 'I've been to Ten-acre Field,' John said. 'He's not there.'

'We'll have to start without him then,' Aunt Sally put in. She lifted up a knife. 'I'll cut the cake. One big bit for me and two little bits for you because . . .'

But Sue stopped her before she could get near the cake. 'You can't start someone's birthday party if the someone isn't there, Aunt Sally.'

'You can if it's an ignorant stupid scarecrow who hasn't got the good manners to turn up,' answered Aunt Sally, sniffily.

John only just managed to keep his temper. 'The reason Worzel isn't here is because he doesn't know about all this. It's a surprise party.'

'Yes,' Sue added, 'and the reason it's a surprise party is because *you* refused to go to the party that Worzel was going to give, Aunt Sally.'

Aunt Sally made a face. The party Worzel had been going to give was nothing like as good as this one. How could anyone expect her to eat potatoes and pigswill?

John turned to Sue. 'We'll have to go and find Worzel. I'll look in the woods.'

'And I'll try the village,' Sue replied.

They both turned back to Aunt Sally. Her eyes were glued on the birthday cake. 'I'll stay here and wait,' she said, as innocently as she could, 'in case he turns up.'

'No you won't!' John exclaimed crossly.

'We're not leaving you here with all this,' Sue put in. 'You can come with me.'

She took Aunt Sally's arm very firmly and dragged her towards the door of the barn. Aunt Sally took one last, longing look at the cake. 'Nasty distrustful children,' she muttered.

Then they all went off in search of Worzel.

Chapter Ten

It was late afternoon. The Crowman was back home after his cup of tea in the village, and hard at work. He was making a new scarecrow, which was going to be called Saggy Farrow. The scarecrow was nearly finished apart from its head and the Crowman held in his hand the large turnip he was going to use for it. He eyed it thoughtfully.

'Season follows season and birthdays come and go for us all,' he said. 'It'll be this scarecrow's birthday next, just as soon as I've made his head for him.'

There was a sound of weeping. Worzel Gummidge stood nearby, watching the Crowman and crying his eyes out. As always, when things got too much for him, and Aunt Sally in particular, Worzel turned to the man who had made him.

'It ain't *just* my birthday,' he grumbled. 'It's my bestest one. Leastways, it's supposed to be. But it's turnin' out to be the worstest I ever 'ad. I ain't 'ad not one single present and not so much as a cup o' tea an' a slice o' cake nowheres.' Worzel burst into tears again.

The Crowman sighed. 'If tea's your only problem, Worzel, you can have that here with me. Anything to stop you crying like that.'

' 'Ave my birthday tea with you, your eminence?' Worzel's eyes lighted up. 'What kind o' cake you got?'

'All kinds,' the Crowman replied. 'I did some baking this afternoon.' He had not approved of the sticky and sickly cakes Miss Maple's tea shop offered and had decided, when he got home, to bake some of his own. He now crossed to a cupboard and lifted out some appetizing country cakes. 'Look,' he said. 'Buttermilk Cake. Rhubarb Gingerbread. Beadle Plum Cake.'

Just the sight of them cheered Worzel up. But the Crowman paused before he cut a slice of any of the cakes for Worzel.

'Shouldn't you be spending your best birthday with those two young friends of yours?' he asked.

Worzel wrinkled his nose. 'Them there titchy yewmans ain't no friends o' mine,' he scoffed. 'Ain't set eyes on 'em for ages.' And, indeed, since the day before when the children had gone off to the village, Worzel hadn't seen them.

'You haven't seen them because they've been planning a surprise birthday party for you,' the Crowman explained. Even if he hadn't seen the children buying the cake, he would have heard about the party from all the scarecrows in the fields around the village.

'Well, that shows 'ow stoopid yewmans are,' said Worzel indignantly. 'They never told me nothin' about it.'

'It's a *surprise* party, Worzel,' the Crowman explained patiently. 'They're probably looking for you now.' He looked sternly at Worzel, who was still crying now and then and wiping his eyes on his sleeve. 'You've been feeling so sorry for yourself, Worzel, you never gave a thought to the fact that others might be thinking up ways of cheering you up. The party's in Scatterbrook Barn. Don't you think you ought to go?'

Worzel gazed longingly at the Crowman's tasty country cakes. He didn't want to leave them uneaten. 'You wouldn't 'appen to know what kind o' eatables they got laid on down there?' he asked the Crowman.

'Crisps, I believe,' answered the Crowman. 'And potted beef sandwiches. Also, I understand, a birthday cake bought and paid for with their saved-up pocket money.'

Worzel wiped away his tears. The party sounded

promising but he still didn't want to go if it meant missing the Crowman's cakes. 'Cripsies, eh?' he said thoughtfully. 'I likes a cripsie. An' sangwidges. An' birthday cake. Only cripsies ain't as nice as Buttermilk Cake is they? An' sangwidges ain't as good as Beadle Plum Cake.' Worzel was in two minds. 'But there ain't nothin' in the world to touch birthday cake,' he continued, 'not unless it's Rhubarb Gingerbread.' He shook his head. 'My oh my, your excellence, fancy them two little 'uns goin' to all that trouble for ol' Worzel.' But he'd decided he was better off where he was. 'Pity really,' he ended, ' 'but I reckon it's every scarecrow's duty to spend 'is Bestest Birthday in 'is Maker's house.'

The Crowman had waited quietly. 'Even,' he now asked, 'when Aunt Sally is in Scatterbrook Barn?'

Worzel stared. 'Aunt Sally, your honour, at ol' Worzel's Bestest Birthday Party?'

The Crowman nodded. 'So I am told.'

'Why, she told me she wouldn't be seen dead at my birthday party,' Worzel replied in amazement. 'Not even if all 'er 'inges rusted an' she'd fallen into tiny pieces.'

'Aunt Sally does what she likes,' the Crowman remarked. 'Not only does she change her own mind when she chooses, she also completely muddles yours. But she *is* at the children's party.'

The mention of Aunt Sally made Worzel change his mind immediately. 'If you'll forgive me, your magnificence,' he said, 'seein' as 'ow them titchy yewmans 'as gone to all that trouble, I thinks it might

be best if I got going to that Bestest Birthday Party.'
And, with only a very short bow to the Crowman,
Worzel left his house and hurried off.

The Crowman shook his head sadly as he watched
him go. 'A happy birthday, Worzel,' he said, 'but I
doubt whether you'll have one.'

*

Worzel was breathless from running when he got
to Scatterbrook Barn and pulled the door open. But
he was in for a big disappointment. What he saw
when he entered was an empty table. All the delicious
things he'd been told about were gone. And behind
the table sat Aunt Sally, looking very pleased with
herself. And very full. The cream round her mouth
told Worzel everything.

'Aunt Sally,' he said in a shocked voice, 'you've
eaten all of my Bestest Birthday Party.'

Aunt Sally said nothing. It was John who spoke.
The children had been standing in the shadows, too
angry with Aunt Sally to speak. 'It wasn't our fault,'
John said.

'She gave me the slip and got back here first,' Sue
added glumly.

' 'Ow could you do it to me, Aunt Sally?' Worzel
asked. 'To ol' Worzel as loves you best in all the
world?'

'If you really loved me, you'd lay down your life
for me,' Aunt Sally replied, licking her lips. 'That's
what brave men do.'

Worzel remembered the brave head and the fight

with the Colonel. 'So I would lay down my life for you, Aunt Sally,' he said. 'But layin' down my birthday cake, that just ain't on.' He looked sadly at the empty table. 'Did my cake 'ave icing all over it an' was there different kinds o' cream inside?'

The children nodded.

'It was all right, for what it was,' Aunt Sally commented, still licking her lips.

'I think you're selfish and cruel, Aunt Sally,' Sue said, trying to keep her temper.

'Never mind, Worzel,' said John, trying to make the best of things. 'You can still have your own birthday party. Mr Braithwaite's got stacks of apples. And there are lots of nuts back in our caravan.'

Worzel screwed up his face in disgust. 'Nuts an' apples? With you three titchy yewmans?' Worzel felt cheated. '*I'm* goin' back to the Crowman's house. For Beadle Plum Cake. An' Rhubarb Gingerbread.'

'But what about us?' John asked. 'We've spent all our pocket money on your party.'

Worzel's head was too full of the feast back at the Crowman's. 'You best do the same as me,' he told the children. 'Look after yourselves.' He went up to Aunt Sally and looked threateningly at her. 'I'll kick you up an' down the 'Igh Street later,' he said.

With those words, Worzel left the barn and started to run back towards the Crowman's house. At least there'd be something nice for his birthday there. The children watched him go. They felt sad and disappointed. After all their trouble, not one word of thanks. And what had happened hadn't been their fault.

Chapter Eleven

Worzel was completely worn out by the time he got back to the Crowman's house. His straw legs were aching. The only thing that kept him going on his long run was the thought of the delicious country cakes lying on the Crowman's table.

Worzel staggered into the Crowman's house more dead than alive. The Crowman was seated at the table in a big wooden chair.

'Back again?' he asked. 'How was your birthday party, Worzel?'

'After givin' it a lot o' thought,' Worzel replied, panting for breath, 'I decided that I owed it to you to spend my Bestest Birthday with you.'

The Crowman had a strange look in his eye. 'That's very kind of you, Worzel. But I'm afraid your stomach won't be any too happy. There's nothing left.'

For the first time, Worzel looked at the table. All it had on it were empty plates. Not a trace of cake. Not a crumb of Buttermilk Cake. Or Beadle Plum Cake. Or Rhubarb Gingerbread. Nothing. Worzel couldn't believe his eyes.

Then he looked up and saw, seated at the other end of the table, the new scarecrow, Saggy Farrow.

'You see, Worzel,' the Crowman explained, 'after

you left, I got to work and finished Saggy Farrow. I put on his head and breathed life into him. He's just enjoying his Being Born Party.'

Worzel gaped. 'That there new-borned scarecrow ain't eaten all that there cake, 'as 'e, your 'onour? Not all at one go?'

The Crowman nodded. 'Have you quite forgotten being born, Worzel. The joy? The hunger? The need to fill up all the empty holes in the loosely packed straw in your body?'

Worzel shook his head. It was a very long time ago and his memory was bad at the best of times. All he could think of was the fact that Saggy Farrow had eaten *all* the cakes.

'You *ought* to remember, Worzel,' the Crowman continued. 'Being Born Day is the greatest day of a scarecrow's life.' He paused. 'And I want you to wish Saggy Farrow a happy Being Born Day.'

'What? *Me?* Wish *'im?*' Worzel exclaimed. 'That greedy object oo's eaten all the cakes? I couldn't do it, sir. Never. I . . .' But Worzel's voice trailed away. The Crowman had risen threateningly from his chair and now spoke in a strong firm voice.

'Worzel! I am the Crowman. I made you and I have now made Saggy Farrow. You are both scarecrows and therefore brothers to the straw. You will wish him a happy Being Born Day.'

'But it ain't fair,' Worzel protested, despite his fear of the Crowman. ' 'Tis my birthday too an' I ain't never 'ad an unhappier day in my life. I ain't 'ad no cake an' I ain't 'ad no present an' not one nice thing 'as 'appened to me all day. It ain't no Bestest Birthday at all. It's the worstest one I've ever 'ad!'

'Worzel Gummidge!' The Crowman spoke more fiercely still. 'You have had more birthdays than any beast or creature under the sun. And still you refuse to learn. Birthdays are never best when they are entered into selfishly. Birthdays are most enjoyed when they are *shared*. Share yours with Saggy Farrow.'

Worzel did not find it easy to say the words but in the end he managed to get them out. 'A very 'appy Bein' Born Day, Saggy Farrow,' he said quietly.

There was a pause. Saggy Farrow was having difficulty in speaking, but not for the same reason as Worzel. Saggy Farrow was so newly born that he'd never spoken before. At last the squeaky sound of his voice came out. 'A 'appy Bestest Birthday, Worzel Gummidge.'

Even Worzel was touched. 'Well now, Mr Crowman, sir,' he said, almost breaking into a smile. 'Them's the first words 'e ever said an' they's about ol' Worzel.'

And then a very surprising thing happened. The moment that Worzel started to smile and to think well of Saggy Farrow, scarecrows started to appear. All sorts of scarecrows. Coming from out of the shadows and all the corners of the Crowman's house. Coming from the cupboards. Coming from everywhere. And all of them carrying parcels. Not very well-wrapped parcels because scarecrows don't have very neat hands, but parcels nevertheless. And when they were all out of hiding, they bowed a special scarecrow bow and said together in a loud voice:

'A Very Happy Bestest Birthday, Worzel! A Very Happy Being Born Day, Saggy Farrow!'

It was difficult to know whether Worzel or Saggy was more surprised and delighted.

'Me oh my,' Worzel said, looking round. 'I never knowed I 'ad so many friends.' He turned to Saggy Farrow. 'That's Scarecrow bowin', that's what that is, Saggy, that they just done. Now you an' me 'as to do some bowin' back. You watch ol' Worzel an' learn from him.'

And Worzel did some very complicated bowing as scarecrows are supposed to do on special occasions. Saggy did his best to imitate Worzel and, considering it was the first time he'd ever bowed, he did very well indeed.

'You does learn fast,' Worzel said, encouragingly. 'Me an' you's sharin' this 'ere birthday a fair ol' treat.'

'What about sharing more birthday cake?' said a voice. It was Aunt Sally, who'd followed Worzel with the children. John and Sue now wished Worzel a happy Bestest Birthday and, for the first time, he thanked them for what they'd done. But Aunt Sally had more important things to think of. 'There *is* going to be another birthday cake, I hope,' she said to the Crowman, licking her lips.

The Crowman nodded and gave a sign. Some of the scarecrows pulled back a screen and there behind it was the biggest and tastiest-looking birthday cake Worzel had ever seen. He pulled Saggy Farrow forward so that they could both take a better look.

'Well, well, that's a cake an' a half, is that one,' said Worzel in wonder. 'In fact it's more than a cake an' a half. It's a cake an' a quarter, that one is!'

'It hasn't got any candles,' John whispered to Sue.

Worzel heard him. 'Candles?' he exclaimed. 'Why for should it 'ave candles on? Dangerous things they is. Set a scarecrow's straw on fire so they would. Why's the cake want candles?'

'So you can blow them out,' Sue explained.

To Worzel that made no sense at all. 'Why for should you light 'em up in the first place then? If all you're going to do is blow 'em out? Daft yewman things.'

The Crowman stopped them arguing. 'Human traditions are not scarecrow traditions,' he explained. 'Humans blow out birthday candles. Scarecrows always dance the Birthday Cake-Walk.

'So take your partners,' the Crowman told all the scarecrows as he produced his battered old fiddle, so that he could play while the others danced. All the scarecrows chose their partners for the Birthday Cake-Walk in great excitement. Worzel turned to Aunt Sally and offered her his arm. She took it, feeling unusually kindly towards Worzel now that there

94

was a chance of a second birthday cake. But, at the same time, Saggy Farrow, who was copying every-thing that Worzel did, took Aunt Sally's other arm. Being so newly born, he didn't know anybody else, and he was the only scarecrow left without a partner.

'You let go of that there arm, Saggy Farrow,' Worzel said crossly, forgetting all his earlier good behaviour. 'Else I'll tear it off 'er body an' 'it you about your 'ead with it!'

'Now, now, Worzel,' the Crowman said, 'that's *not* the spirit. Sharing, Worzel, remember, sharing.'

Worzel made a big effort and controlled himself. 'Yes, your importanceship,' he said, 'whatever you says.' He let Saggy take Aunt Sally's other arm and they joined the other scarecrows.

Then the Crowman started to play his fiddle and the Birthday Cake-Walk began. John and Sue watched in delight as the scarecrows flung them-selves into the dance, which involved a lot of mad turning about and swinging of straw arms. And they forgot about all the trouble that Aunt Sally had given them and how ungrateful Worzel had been.

After the dance, the birthday cake was served. And Worzel made sure that everyone had a piece, even John and Sue. And Aunt Sally enjoyed herself so much that she didn't mind not getting the whole cake to herself. And everyone tucked into the cake and again wished Saggy Farrow and Worzel Gum-midge a happy birthday.

The party went on well into the evening. And by the time it was over, even Worzel Gummidge had to admit it was the bestest Bestest Birthday he had ever had.